WHEN LOLLIPOP LADIES

ATTACK!

When Lollipop Ladies Attack! by Vicki Englund
Published by *Australian eBook Publisher*
Text copyright © Vicki Englund 2014
Illustrations copyright © Nicky Johnston 2014

Ebook Version
1st Edition 2014, ePub and Mobi
eISBN: 978-1-925177-50-3
Ebook creation: Converted from digital source file
Ebook files created and distributed by: *Australian eBook Publisher*
www.AustralianEbookPublisher.com.au

Print Version
1st Edition 2014, pbk.
ISBN: 978-1-925177-51-0
Typeset in: 22/28 Bangle Font

National Library of Australia Cataloguing-in-Publication entry

Target Audience: For primary school age.
Subjects: Traffic safety and children--Juvenile fiction.
Other Authors/Contributors: Johnston, Nicky, 1971- illustrator.
Dewey Number: A823.4

Written by Vicki Englund
www.vickienglund.com.au

Illustrated by Nicky Johnston
www.nickyjohnston.com.au

WHEN LOLLIPOP LADIES

ATTACK!

Vicki Englund

Illustrated by Nicky Johnston

CHAPTER ONE

'I'm the new Lollipop Lady,' says Mum.

'Great!' I say. 'What flavour lollipop do I get first?'

Mum gives me one of her looks. 'Not that kind of lollipop, Abby.'

I know this already.
I was just hoping it
wasn't true.

It's going to be so
embarrassing! My
mum is going to be the
Lollipop Lady at school!
And she starts next
Monday morning. How
will I ever show my face?

My best friend Milly's
mum is a doctor. My
other best friend Cleo's
mum owns a shoe shop.

Other people's mums do important things.

Mum must have read my mind. The next thing she says is, 'Being a Lollipop Lady is a very important job.'

I look guilty. 'Who said it wasn't?'

All I got for that was another one of Mum's looks.

Oh please, can Monday morning never come?

4

CHAPTER TWO

It's Monday morning – Mum's first day at work. At my school! I take longer than usual to get dressed.

'Hurry up, Abby,' Mum says. 'I have to be there early every day now.'

Does she have to rub it in? No sleep-ins on school days ever!

'Mum?' I ask. 'Are you sure you want to be a Lollipop Lady?'

Mum suddenly looks quite proud. 'My real title is School Crossing Supervisor.'

I feel a bit better about that. School Crossing Supervisor sounds way less embarrassing than Lollipop Lady.

We get to school. Mum's wearing a long yellow coat with a bright orange stripe and a bright orange hat. She's almost glowing! And there's the lollipop sign saying 'STOP' – bright orange too!

Everyone stares at her. Then at me. Then at her. Oh no, here comes Milly.

Milly's mum smiles at my mum. 'Good morning, Coralie. Don't you look smart?'

'Thanks, Suzi,' Mum replies.

Mum looks right, left, then right again. There are no cars too close. She walks out into the middle of the road. She puts up the STOP sign. Then the worst part – she blows a whistle.

Suzi, Milly and I walk across the crossing.

'Thanks, Coralie,' Milly calls out. Milly turns to me and says, 'It must be so cool having a mum who's a Lollipop Lady.'

'Must it?' I ask.

Then I think about it – this is going to happen every day!

10

CHAPTER THREE

After school, I wait
to cross the road. Mum
looks right, left, then
right again. She walks
out. Then, I don't know
why, but I start walking
after her. I guess I'm just
used to following her.

'Abby!' Mum yells it really loudly. Everyone looks at me. 'Wait for me to blow the whistle before you cross, please!'

She blows the whistle. I give her my best dirty look. Everyone starts to cross.

This is the most embarrassing day of my life! I want the stupid crossing to open up and swallow me. Then I'd

never have to face my
friends again.

I walk with Cleo and
her mum to their house
for a play date. Cleo has
two new pairs of shoes
in her bedroom. That's
what you get if your
mum owns a shoe shop.

Last week, Milly had
a new medicine cup
with a picture of a cute
kitten on it. That's what
you get if your mum is a
doctor.

What do I get for having a mum who's a Lollipop Lady? Yelled at in front of everyone, that's what!

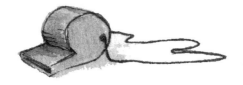

CHAPTER FOUR

On Tuesday, I
remember to wait until
Mum blows the whistle.
But Hugo Harris doesn't
wait. His right foot
steps off the footpath
and Mum glares at him.
'Hugo! Wait for the
whistle to blow, please.'

Oh well, I'm not
the only one the new
Lollipop Lady yells at.

'Your mum is so
mean,' Hugo sneers
at me. 'And anyway,
she's just a Lollipop
Lady. My mum's an op--
an optom-- She tests
people's eyes.'

What can I say? Mum
is just a Lollipop Lady,
even if you call it School
Crossing Supervisor. It's

16

not important like being an optometrist.

At home, things aren't much better. Mum acts like she's a Lollipop Lady all the time now.

I kick off my shoes in the living room. I hear a whistle blow. It's Mum! 'Don't leave those lying there for people to trip over,' she says. I'm so shocked I just pick them up.

Then tonight, I'm telling Dad about coming second in my one hundred metres running race. Suddenly, we hear a whistle blow from the bathroom. 'Abby!' Mum calls.

I go into the bathroom. Mum points to my netball shirt lying on the floor. 'Does this belong here?'

I want to say, 'You know it doesn't.'

Instead, I just pick it up.
I feel like hiding that
whistle. My mum has
gone crazy with power!
What will she do next?

CHAPTER FIVE

Wednesday morning,
Mum looks right, left,
then right again. There
are no cars too close.
Mum walks into the
middle of the road. Her
coat is so bright I think
you must be able to see

her from space! Will I ever get used to this?

She holds up her bright orange STOP sign. She puts her whistle in her mouth about to blow it. Then…

Whoosh! A car speeds right past! It goes really close to Mum who is so surprised she doesn't even blow her whistle.

Everyone else's mouth drops open in shock. That's not supposed to happen.

We all look at the Lollipop Lady. She looks like she might explode. 'Someone write down that car's number plate!' Mum calls out.

Hugo Harris fumbles in his bag. He brings out a notebook – it looks like his big slobbery dog has chewed it. Then a pencil. But it's too late. The car has gone.

'Never mind, Hugo,' Mum smiles. 'Thanks anyway. At least we

know it's a silver station wagon. I'll be keeping my eye out for that.'

Hugo gives a big grin. 'Your mum's not so bad after all,' he says after we cross over.

'At least she picked on a driver today,' I say. 'Instead of us.'

One thing's for sure – the driver of that silver station wagon better watch out!

CHAPTER SIX

Thursday morning, and I have to get up early... again. Having a mum who's a Lollipop Lady is making me lose sleep!

'That silver station wagon better stop

today,' says Mum. She puts on her bright yellow vest.

'What will you do if it doesn't?' I ask.

'Report it. I'm a School Crossing Supervisor. It's my duty to keep the kids safe.'

Mum sounded very serious. I guess her job is kind of important after all. Important but still a bit embarrassing.

At school, Mum's bright orange hat goes on. She grabs her bright orange STOP sign.

Mum looks right, left, then right again. There are no cars too close. She walks out onto the crossing. She's about to blow the whistle. Suddenly...

That silver station wagon seems to come from nowhere. It's going really fast!

Mum looks worried. What will she do?

'Stay there, kids!' she calls out. We all stay. We've learnt very quickly to obey the new Lollipop Lady.

Mum faces the silver station wagon. She holds up her big STOP sign. She blows her whistle. The driver slams on the brakes and the car stops.

Mum calls out, 'Can't you see the STOP sign?'

The man gives her a nasty look. 'Out of my way, I'm in a hurry.'

'But it's my job to make sure these children cross the road safely,' Mum says.

The man looks even nastier. 'Some of us have got important work to do.'

Uh-oh. Did he mean the Lollipop Lady's job isn't important?

Mum's nostrils grow bigger. I'm expecting smoke to come out of them. She walks up to the driver. She lifts up her STOP sign. What's she doing? Is she going to hit the man?

He looks scared. He quickly starts to drive away. Mum bumps the

back of the car with her
STOP sign.

'You need to learn
some manners!' she
calls out.

'You're crazy, lady!'
the man yells out the
window. Then he's gone.

Back at the crossing,
nobody dares to move.

CHAPTER SEVEN

The new Lollipop Lady is a hero! Did I mention she's my mum?

All week, kids keep coming up to me.

Some say, 'Your mum rocks!'

Others say, 'That Lollipop Lady is so cool!'

One even says, 'Coralie for Prime Minister!'

But one thing's for sure. They all agree – Mum. Is. A. LEGEND!

The man in the silver station wagon got into big trouble. He has to pay a fine of three hundred dollars for dangerous driving.

But he told the police what Mum did. Lollipop

Ladies aren't supposed
to bump cars with their
STOP signs. Mum has to
go to a class. It's called:
'MANAGE YOUR ANGER'.
She's going to learn how
not to lose her temper
on the job. I hope she
can put it into practice
at home.

Our local newspaper
story says, 'Hero
Lollipop Lady, Coralie,
protects the kids of
Bonny Lea State School'.

The headline in huge letters reads, 'WHEN LOLLIPOP LADIES ATTACK!' Everyone thinks that's pretty funny.

There's a photo too. Hugo Harris took it with his dad's phone. In it, Mum is bumping the silver station wagon with the STOP sign. She looks kind of scary. But at least the story says that she was only doing her job. She just got a bit carried away.

Mum's calmed down a bit at home now. What a relief! No more whistles blowing when I leave something on the floor.

I'm really proud of my mum. Lollipop Lady... School Crossing Supervisor... whatever anyone else calls her, I get to call her the best name of all – Mum!

Vicki Englund has loved writing stories since she was a child. She does this through TV and film scripts, books and journalism. *When Lollipop Ladies Attack!* is her first published children's book. Vicki lives in Brisbane, Australia, with her husband and daughter... and yes, she has a cat. (Don't all writers have a cat?) They also have two fussy chickens called Betty and Veronica.

www.vickienglund.com.au

A big hello to Coralie, the real-life former lollipop lady who always had a smile for the children and never went crazy with power.

Nicky Johnston is a children's book author and illustrator from Melbourne, Australia. She lives with her husband and four sons who often feature in her books. Nicky is a primary school educator who loves to teach children to draw and paint. School visits are the highlight of her work.

www.nickyjohnston.com.au

(Author/illustrator of *Go Away, Mr Worrythoughts!*, *Happythoughts are Everywhere...*, *Actually, I can*)

Printed in Australia
AUOC02n0803021014
263552AU00001B/1/P